The Bumper Book of Christmas Stories

©1991 Grandreams Limited

Sam's Special Sandwiches, The Little Toy Theatre, The King Who Cancelled Christmas, The Nativity Play, The No-Snowman, The Dog Who Fetched Father Christmas written by Valerie Hall. *Jimmy And The New Year, Frost Pictures, Santa's Best Coat, Wildlife In Winter, Santa's Ride, North Wind, Simon's Special Snowman, Snow For Christmas* written by Beryl Johnston. *A Christmas Carol, The Nutcracker, The Little Fir Tree* re-told by Anne McKie.

Illustrations by Linden Artists: *Endpapers, The Little Toy Theatre, Santa's Ride, Wildlife In Winter, The Nativity Play, The King Who Cancelled Christmas, Jimmy And The New Year, North Wind.* Russell and Russell: *Frost Pictures, Simon's Special Snowman, The Dog Who Fetched Father Christmas, The No-Snowman, Santa's Best Coat.* Associated Freelance Artists: *Snow For Christmas, Sam's Special Sandwiches.*
Ken McKie: *Cover, A Christmas Carol, The Nutcracker, The Little Fir Tree, The Night Before Christmas, The Twelve Days of Christmas.*

This edition published 1995

Published by
Grandreams Limited
Jadwin House, 205-211 Kentish Town Road, London, NW5 2JU.

Printed in Czech Rebublic

CB1

Contents

This classic Christmas story written
by Charles Dickens, takes place in London
during the reign of Queen Victoria.
Ebenezer Scrooge is known to everyone
as a mean and unkind man.
Then late one Christmas Eve, the ghost of
his old partner Jacob Marley appears
and warns him that he must change his ways...

Ebenezer
Scrooge

Tiny Tim
Cratchit

Bob Cratchit

The Ghost of
Jacob Marley

The Spirit of
Christmas Past

The Spirit of
Christmas Present

The Spirit of
Christmas
To Come

A CHRISTMAS CAROL

Re-told by Anne McKie.
Illustrated by Ken McKie.

Once upon a time - on Christmas Eve - Ebenezer Scrooge sat busy in his counting-house.

A faded sign hung above his office door that read: "Scrooge and Marley". Jacob Marley had been Scrooge's business partner, but he had died over seven years ago, and Scrooge was such an old skinflint he wouldn't pay for a new sign to be put up.

It was cold, bleak, biting weather that day and the thick fog outside came pouring in through every chink and keyhole. But Scrooge never felt the winter chill, for he was a mean, tight-fisted old miser with a heart as cold as ice. He never did a kind deed or helped anyone, although he had piles of money locked away . . . and most of all he hated CHRISTMAS!

All day long Scrooge left his office door wide open to keep his eye on his clerk, Bob Cratchit, even on Christmas Eve. The poor fellow was so cold he had to work in his coat and scarf. And the fire Scrooge allowed him to have was so small it looked like one coal.

"A Merry Christmas, Uncle!" cried a cheerful voice. It was Scrooge's nephew, Fred, who had called to wish him the very best for the festive season.

"Bah!" cried Scrooge. "Humbug!"

"Don't be angry, Uncle. Come and share Christmas dinner with us tomorrow," said his nephew kindly.

The very word CHRISTMAS made Scrooge angry. "If I had my way," shouted Scrooge, "every idiot who goes around wishing people 'Merry Christmas', should be boiled with his own Christmas pudding and buried with a stake of holly through his heart. Keep Christmas in your own way and let me keep it in mine!" And Scrooge pointed to the door.

As he left, Fred stopped to wish Bob Cratchit a 'Merry Christmas'. The poor man was trying to warm his freezing hands by a candle flame.

The afternoon got foggier and darker and colder. A little boy bent down to sing a carol at Scrooge's keyhole, but at the first few notes of:

"God rest you, merry gentlemen,
May nothing you dismay!"

Scrooge grabbed his ruler and the poor boy fled in terror.

At last the time came to stop work and close the office. Bob Cratchit blew out his candle and put on his hat.

"I suppose you want all day off tomorrow," snapped Scrooge.

"If that's alright, sir," said Bob Cratchit timidly. "It's only once a year, and it is Christmas Day!"

"It is not alright!" replied Scrooge. "Just remember that I will have to pay you a whole day's wage for no work!" and Scrooge left with a growl.

Bob Cratchit locked up the office in a twinkling. On the way home - just because it was Christmas - he went down an icy slide twenty times, just for the fun of it!

Scrooge, on the other hand, ate his supper all alone at a nearby inn, and went home to bed.

He lived by himself in a dark old house that had once belonged to his partner, Jacob Marley.

Now, that Christmas Eve, as Scrooge put his key in the lock, he looked up, and instead of the brass door-knocker, he saw Marley's face!

As Scrooge stared in amazement, it turned into a door-knocker again.

At once Scrooge unlocked his door, and hurried inside and quickly lit a candle. Then he took a good look around all the rooms, just to make sure no-one was there. He even looked under the bed!

Quite satisfied, he locked his bedroom door and put on his dressing gown, his slippers and nightcap.

All of a sudden, an old bell that hung by the fireplace began to swing to and fro. Soon it began to ring out loudly - and so did every bell in the house.

Then Scrooge heard a different sound, as if someone was dragging heavy chains from the cellar, up the stairs and into his bedroom.

Poor Scrooge's knees began to knock and his teeth began to chatter as JACOB MARLEY'S GHOST floated through the door!

At first Scrooge thought his eyes were playing tricks, or his supper had given him indigestion. But the ghost did look like his old friend Jacob Marley, although it was covered from head to foot in chains, and loaded down with heavy cash-boxes, bunches of keys and big metal padlocks.

"I have come to warn you, Ebenezer Scrooge," wailed the ghost, "before it's too late!" And he rattled his chains at Scrooge.

"If you do not mend your ways at once, and become kind, loving and give to other people, you will end up like me!" the ghost went on. "In my life I cared for nothing but money. And look at me now. A lonely old ghost, deemed to wander around with nothing but money-boxes for company!"

Scrooge shuddered. "Tell me, dear friend, how can I change?"

By now the ghost was floating towards the window, his voice fading. "You will be visited by three Spirits when the clock strikes one. Listen to them, Ebenezer Scrooge, and you will escape my fate!"

And with that, the ghost of Jacob Marley floated out into the dark night and vanished among the chimney pots.

Feeling very tired, Scrooge closed the window, crept into bed and fell fast asleep.

A nearby clock struck midnight and Scrooge woke up. Feeling very nervous he lay awake until one. Would he see the first of the three Spirits - or had it all been a bad dream?

On the stroke of one, light filled the room. The curtains of his bed were drawn back and Scrooge found himself face to face with a ghost! It was a very strange ghost, small like a child, with long white hair.

"Who or what are you?" asked Scrooge.

"I am the Ghost of Christmas Past," said the Spirit in a gentle voice. "I am here to remind you of your past!"

The Spirit whisked Scrooge, still in his dressing gown and slippers, up in the air and out into the dark night . . . and back in time!

The city had vanished and they found themselves in a little country town. Scrooge was a boy again surrounded by his school friends.

All the boys were going home for the Christmas holidays. Sad to say, no-one came to fetch young Ebenezer that year. So he was left alone at school to spend a miserable Christmas all by himself.

When Scrooge remembered this he began to cry. The Spirit smiled and waved his hand. "Let us see another Christmas!"

Scrooge saw himself sitting in the schoolroom a few years later. Again all his friends had gone home for the Christmas holiday.

Suddenly, the door opened and his beloved sister, Fran, darted in. She flung her arms round his neck and kissed him.

"I have come to bring you home! Not just for the holidays, but for ever and ever!"

Quick as a flash, the Spirit whisked Scrooge away from his old school. In no time at all they were outside a warehouse door and the Spirit asked Scrooge if he knew the place.

"Know it! I was an apprentice there!" cried Scrooge excitedly.

They went in. Scrooge could see himself as a young gentleman, having a marvellous time at the office Christmas party.

His old boss, Mr. Fezziwig, had ordered all his young apprentices to stop work and join the family in fun and games. There was music and dancing and presents for all.

Poor Scrooge remembered how happy he had been in those days, but now he cared more about money than friends. And he had forgotten how to have fun.

The Spirit of Christmas Past had made Scrooge see what a lonely miserable old man he had become.

Suddenly Scrooge realised that he was back in his own bedroom. Tired out, he fell fast asleep.

All too soon he was awakened in the middle of a huge snore by a clock striking one.

As he peered over the bedclothes, Scrooge saw the whole place filled with rosy light from the next room.

Trembling, he got up and shuffled in his slippers to the door.

"Come in! Come in!" boomed a voice. "I am the Spirit of Christmas Present! Come in and get to know me!"

Scrooge entered timidly, and what a sight met his eyes. The room was full to bursting with Christmas fayre. And right in the middle sat a cheery fat giant of a ghost.

"Touch my robe!" said the Spirit of Christmas Present.

Scrooge did as he was told and held on tight.

Everything in the room vanished and Scrooge found himself walking through the cold snowy city streets together with the Spirit.

It was Christmas morning and the shops were still open. The grocer's, the baker's, the poulterer's and the fruit shops. All selling Christmas food right up to the very last minute.

Church bells rang out all over the city, calling folks to church. The streets were full of happy bustling people. Some going to worship, while others were carrying their Christmas goose to the baker's - to be cooked in his huge ovens; everyone looking forward to their Christmas dinner.

Quickly the Spirit moved on with Scrooge still hanging tight on to his robe. At last they stopped and slipped, quite unseen, into the home of Scrooge's clerk, Bob Cratchit.

Now this poor fellow had to bring up his family on fifteen shillings a week, for that was all that mean old Scrooge would pay him.

But today it was Christmas Day, and Mrs Cratchit had managed to save enough to make a Christmas dinner - a special dinner that all the Cratchits would remember until next Christmas.

As Scrooge and the Spirit gazed at the happy scene, Mrs Cratchit was busy laying the table for dinner helped by her daughters, while a couple of the younger Cratchits danced round the room getting very excited.

Young Peter was in charge of a great pan of potatoes, bubbling away on the fire. Everybody was simply longing for dinner time.

"Here's Father coming home," cried the two little Cratchits, as Bob came home from church with his son, Tiny Tim, on his shoulder.

Young Tiny Tim was very frail. He had to use a little crutch, and could only walk with an iron frame strapped onto his leg. When he was tired he sat by the fire on his own small stool.

In rushed the young Cratchits carrying the goose that had been roasting in the baker's oven. It was dinner time at last!

The dishes were put on the table and grace was said. Everyone took a deep breath as Mrs Cratchit plunged her carving knife into the hot roast goose, stuffed with sage and onion and served with apple sauce and mashed potatoes. It was enough for the whole family.

Great excitement now as Mrs Cratchit left the room.

She returned, quite flushed, with a Christmas pudding. And what a pudding! It was speckled like a cannonball, blazing with brandy and a sprig of holly on top.

At last dinner was finished, and the whole family sat round the fire with roast chestnuts and some punch. Bob raised his glass. "A Merry Christmas to us all, my dears. God bless us!"

"God bless us everyone!" said Tiny Tim, and Bob reached out and held his frail little hand.

"Spirit," said Scrooge, "tell me if Tiny Tim will live!"

"I see an empty chair," replied the Spirit, "and a crutch without an owner. If things do not change, Tiny Tim will die!"

"No, no," said Scrooge. "Kind Spirit, say he will not die!"

Scrooge hung his head as he remembered how little money he paid Bob Cratchit. It was because of him Bob's family were so poor, so shabby and so often cold and hungry.

That night the Spirit of Christmas Present showed Scrooge many things. They visited places that made Scrooge shudder. They flew over bleak dark moors where miners worked underground. They flew over the raging sea and heard sailors singing carols as they steered the ship through a storm.

Worst of all they saw ragged hungry children with no-one to care for them, even at Christmas. It was then Scrooge remembered that he had never tried to help them, although he had been given many chances.

It had seemed such a long night and the Spirit and Scrooge had travelled far. A bell struck twelve and the Spirit vanished.

As Scrooge looked again, he saw a dark figure drifting towards him through the mist.

"Are you the Spirit of the Future?" whispered Scrooge.

The Spirit did not answer, just pointed. He showed Scrooge people talking about a certain old miser who had just died. No-one was sad, no-one went to his funeral, and no-one missed him or loved him.

Then, without a word, the Spirit of the Future took Scrooge to the home of Bob Cratchit. There he saw the sad faces of the young Cratchits, the empty stool by the fireside and the crutch in the corner. Scrooge realised that Tiny Tim must have died.

"Tell me about my future, Spirit!" begged Scrooge trembling, but the Spirit didn't reply. Instead he led him to a churchyard and pointed at a gravestone.

Scrooge crept towards it and written on the stone was his own name: EBENEZER SCROOGE.

"That can't be me!" cried Scrooge. "I will change! I promise to keep Christmas in my heart all the year round!"

As poor frightened Scrooge tried to grab the Spirit's arm, the black robe collapsed and changed into a bedpost.

Yes, the bedpost was his own, the bed was his own and the room was his own. Best of all, he was alive with lots of time in front of him to change his ways.

Scrooge jumped out of bed laughing and crying in the same breath. He rushed round the room dancing and singing, so happy, he put on all his clothes inside out and back to front.

Running to the window, he opened it and stuck his head out. "What day is it today?" he called to a boy dressed in his best clothes.

"Why, Christmas Day!" replied the lad.

"So, I haven't missed it!" said Scrooge to himself.

Then he told the young boy to run and buy the huge turkey hanging in the poulterer's shop, and he gave the boy half-a-crown for his trouble.

"I'll send it to Bob Cratchit!" chuckled Scrooge. "He'll never guess where it came from. It must be twice as big as Tiny Tim!"

Having paid for the turkey and a man with a cab to take it over to Camden Town, Scrooge felt quite breathless.

No time to waste. Scrooge shaved, then dressed himself up in his best clothes. He went out into the streets calling: "Merry Christmas" to passers by and smiling at everyone he met.

He went to the church and then walked towards his nephew Fred's house. He passed the door a dozen times before he plucked up courage to knock.

A girl let him in and Scrooge went straight to the dining room and poked his head round the door.

"Why bless my soul!" cried his nephew, "who's that?"

"It's your uncle Scrooge. I have come to dinner. Will you let me in?"

The family gave Scrooge such a warm welcome that he felt at home in five minutes. He enjoyed a wonderful party with wonderful games - the old man never felt happier.

Next morning, Scrooge wanted to be first at the office (just to catch Bob Cratchit coming in late).

The clock struck nine, no Bob. Scrooge sat with his door wide open. At last at eighteen and a half minutes past nine, Bob arrived.

His hat and scarf were off before he opened the door. He jumped up on his stool and began writing away as fast as he could.

"What do you mean by coming here at this time of day?" growled Scrooge, pretending to be angry.

"It's only once a year!" pleaded poor Bob. "I promise it won't happen again!"

"I'm not going to stand this kind of thing any longer!" Scrooge went on, digging Bob Cratchit in the ribs. "And therefore I am about to raise your salary!"

Bob jumped back.

"A Merry Christmas, Bob," said Scrooge slapping him on the back. "A Merrier Christmas than I've given for many a year. Build up the fire; we'll sit together and talk about your wages and how I can help your family!"

Scrooge was better than his word. He did much more than he promised; and to Tiny Tim, who did not die, he was a second father.

Some people laughed at such a change in Scrooge - but he didn't care a bit.

He had no more visits from ghosts or spirits. And it was always said of him that he knew how to keep Christmas as well as any man alive.

May that be said of all of us. As Tiny Tim said: "God Bless Us, Everyone!"

The ghosts who appeared to Ebenezer Scrooge that Christmas Eve showed him what a mean and horrid old man he was.

By being kind and helping others, he became the happy man that he had been when he was younger.

But did the ghosts really come to him, or was it all just a dream?

Ebenezer Scrooge

Tiny Tim Cratchit

Bob Cratchit

The Ghost of
Jacob Marley

The Spirit of
Christmas Past

The Spirit of
Christmas Present

The Spirit of
Christmas
To Come

The Twelve Days Of Christmas

The first day of Christmas
My true love sent to me
A partridge in a pear tree.

The second day of Christmas
My true love sent to me
Two turtle doves, and
A partridge in a pear tree.

The third day of Christmas
My true love sent to me
Three French hens,
Two turtle doves, and
A partridge in a pear tree.

The fourth day of Christmas
My true love sent to me
Four colly birds,
Three French hens,
Two turtle doves, and
A partridge in a pear tree.

The fifth day of Christmas
My true love sent to me
Five gold rings,
Four colly birds,
Three French hens,
Two turtle doves, and
A partridge in a pear tree.

The sixth day of Christmas
My true love sent to me
Six geese a-laying,
Five gold rings,
Four colly birds,
Three French hens,
Two turtle doves, and
A partridge in a pear tree.

The seventh day of Christmas
My true love sent to me
Seven swans a-swimming,
Six geese a-laying,
Five gold rings,
Four colly birds,
Three French hens,
Two turtle doves, and
A partridge in a pear tree.

The eighth day of Christmas
My true love sent to me
Eight maids a-milking,
Seven swans a-swimming,
Six geese a-laying,
Five gold rings,
Four colly birds,
Three French hens,
Two turtle doves, and
A partridge in a pear tree.

The ninth day of Christmas
My true love sent to me
Nine drummers drumming,
Eight maids a-milking,
Seven swans a-swimming,
Six geese a-laying,
Five gold rings,
Four colly birds,
Three French hens,
Two turtle doves, and
A partridge in a pear tree.

The tenth day of Christmas
My true love sent to me
Ten pipers piping,
Nine drummers drumming,
Eight maids a-milking,
Seven swans a-swimming,
Six geese a-laying,
Five gold rings,
Four colly birds,
Three French hens
Two turtle doves, and
A partridge in a pear tree.

The eleventh day of Christmas
My true love sent to me
Eleven ladies dancing,
Ten pipers piping,
Nine drummers drumming,
Eight maids a-milking,
Seven swans a-swimming,
Six geese a-laying,
Five gold rings,
Four colly birds,
Three French hens,
Two turtle doves, and
A partridge in a pear tree.

The twelfth day of Christmas
My true love sent to me
Twelve lords a-leaping,
Eleven ladies dancing,
Ten pipers piping,
Nine drummers drumming,
Eight maids a-milking,
Seven swans a-swimming,
Six geese a-laying,
Five gold rings,
Four colly birds,
Three French hens,
Two turtle doves, and.........

A partridge in a pear tree.

Wildlife In Winter

It's funny, when you walk around
And think of creatures underground,
So many sleeping safe and sound
In burrow deep or earthy mound.

The badger in his set will sleep
And only out with dusk he'll creep,
The fox into his lair can leap
While hedgehogs tight till Spring will keep;

And stranger when you think, instead,
Of creatures living overhead,
How cosily they lie abed
When trees and bushes look so dead.

The squirrel nestles in his drey.
The owl will slumber through the day
While rooks on higher branches sway
And finches in the thornbush play.

They do not have the kind of heat
We need to warm our hands and feet,
For cosy fur is hard to beat
And feathers are both warm and neat.

They gather leaves with beak and claw
Or bracken dry, with mouth and paw,
To line their dwelling, roof to floor
And keep them safe through Winter raw.

Jimmy and The New Year

It was New Year's Eve and Jimmy and his friends were sledging on Hawthorn Common. Jimmy had a special sledge he'd been given for Christmas, and it went much faster than any of the others.

"Whee!" he shouted as he whizzed down the hill, leaving everyone else far behind. He skidded past a big hawthorn bush and landed in the middle of a soft snowdrift.

"That looks fun. Can I have a ride on your sledge?" asked a small, piping voice. Jimmy sat up in surprise as a little figure in a long white robe crawled out from the bush.

"What are you doing there?"
cried Jimmy.

"Hiding from Father Time,"
came the reply. "I'm the New Year
and I'm supposed to start work at
midnight. But I want to have a bit of
fun first."

"Alright," agreed Jimmy. "Help
me pull the sledge to the top of the
next hill, then we'll slide down the
other side."

When they reached the top, the
New Year sat on the sledge behind
Jimmy. "Hold tight," cried Jimmy, as
the sledge gathered speed.

"This is *tre-men-dous!*"
squeaked the New Year, gasping for
breath as they shot to the bottom of
the steep slope. Then he gave a
squeal and pointed to someone in
the distance. "It's Father Time!"

Coming towards them was an old man with a long beard. He was leaning on a stick and carried an hour-glass in his hand. "If he catches me I'll get a spanking for running away," said the New Year. "I'm off!" and in a moment he had disappeared.

Father Time came trudging through the snow and sat down on a fallen log. "I'll never catch the New Year," he sighed. "He's such a little rascal. He's got to ring the bells in Time Tower at midnight, to let everyone know the new year has begun."

"The New Year ran away because he was afraid he'd get a spanking if you caught him," explained Jimmy. "But if you'll promise to forgive him, I'll try to find him for you."

"Oh, very well," agreed Father Time. "But remember, he's got to be at Time Tower before midnight. Now I'll put a bit of magic on your sledge, so that it will slide up hills as well as down them."

So Father Time waved his hour-glass over the sledge and Jimmy set off to find the New Year.

Very soon he found a trail of small footprints in the deep snow and he followed them up and down the hills on his sledge. "This is great," chuckled Jimmy, as he sped towards the far edge of the Common. "But I hope I can catch up with that little rascal before it gets too late."

Then he heard a cry for help and there on the edge of the Common was the New Year, stuck fast in a barbed wire fence. "I was trying to get through, but my robe caught on the wire and I can't get free," he wailed.

"I'll help you," said Jimmy. "But first you promise to go to Time Tower."

"But Father Time will be cross with me," cried the New Year.

"He told me he'll forgive you if you come straight back with me," said Jimmy.

"Oh, alright, I promise," replied the New Year, sulkily. "But I'll have to ring the New Year Bells, and that's jolly hard work."

Jimmy untangled the New Year from the barbed wire and they both went back to the sledge. This time the New Year sat in front to guide it.

They slid up and down the hills at a great speed and the New Year enjoyed himself so much he was in a much better mood when Time Tower came in sight.

It was a very tall building and at the top, just below the roof, Jimmy could see three big bells.

Down below, Father Time was waiting for them and he was so pleased to see the New Year, he forgot all about being cross with him. "I'll leave the magic on your sledge so that you can get home quickly," he told Jimmy.

So Jimmy raced away over the snow and by the time he reached home, the moon was shining brightly.

He was allowed to stay up late that night, so he stood by the window and listened carefully for the sound of the New Year Bells. At last they rang out in the distance, DING, DANG, DONG. DING, DANG, DONG!

"Happy New Year!" cried Jimmy's Uncle Mac, coming through the door with a lucky lump of coal and a bunch of balloons. Jimmy chuckled and chose one balloon for himself and one for the New Year, just in case he should see him again on Hawthorn Common.

Frost Pictures

In winter, jumping from my bed
To part my curtains, blue and red,
I see upon the windowpane
A frosty fairyland again;

As though a secret, magic hand
Had painted there a wonderland
Of frozen ferns and castles tall,
And sparkling flowers, large and small.

But when the sun begins to rise
With beams so dazzling to my eyes,
The magic pictures quickly pass
And leave just water on the glass.

Sam's Special Sandwiches

When Sam Stevens got home from school he knew right away that something was wrong; his dad's car was in the drive and Dad was never home that early. He threw a breathless "thank you" to the lady who had driven him home and dashed up to the front door. It opened before Sam could ring the bell and Mr. Stevens was standing there, smiling. "Bet you're surprised to see me," he said.

Sam went in, hung up his coat and satchel, and looked round for his mother; she wasn't there. A horrid tingly feeling came into his stomach.

Mr. Stevens crouched down and put his hands on Sam's shoulders.

"Granny's hurt her foot and can't walk very well so Mummy's staying with her for a few days to help out."

"Whew!" sighed Sam, relieved that things weren't as bad as he'd imagined. The tingly feeling in his tummy went away.

"Why don't you go upstairs and wash your hands while I make your tea?" suggested Sam's dad. "And what will M'sewer 'ave?" he asked in a funny accent. "Lobstaire Sooflay? Duck with a beeootiful orange soos? Or plain old Caviar and cheeps?"

Sam laughed and settled for fish fingers and tinned spaghetti. He was well aware that his dad could barely boil an egg.

After tea Sam made his Granny a 'get well' card and then watched TV.

"Bath time, Sam," came a voice from the kitchen. His dad was still trying to clean spaghetti off the bottom of the pan.

Sam was on his way upstairs when he remembered something that brought a funny feeling back into his tummy and sent him hurrying down again.

"What's the matter?" said his dad, as Sam burst into the kitchen.

"Tomorrow. It's the school Christmas party."

His dad frowned. "So?"

"We're all supposed to take something to eat. Mum said she'd make me some sandwiches and a cake."

"I see," said Mr. Stevens, and thought for a minute. "Well I don't know about the cake, but I'm sure I could manage the sandwiches."

"Perhaps I'd better help," said Sam, doubtfully.

"All right then. I'll butter, you spread."

While his dad buttered slices of bread, Sam got out all his favourite fillings; peanut butter, cheese spread, honey, jam and chicken paste. To these he added a jar of gherkins and a jar of little white onions.

With all the buttered bread spread out on the table, Sam went round putting on a bit of this, a bit of that, a gherkin here, an onion there until half the slices were covered. Then he put on the tops.

Mr. Stevens eyed them curiously. "What's in that one?" he asked.

Sam lifted its lid. "Cheese spread, honey and gherkin," he said, proudly.

His dad grinned. "Seeing that they're such *unusual* sandwiches, why don't we cut them into unusual shapes instead of boring old squares and triangles? We could use Mummy's pastry cutters."

Sam thought this was a great idea and when they finished there were hearts, rounds, diamonds and curly shaped sandwiches all over the place.

Inglenook Infants was in a state of high excitement for not only was it the day of the Christmas party, but a very special visitor was coming as well.

Sam carefully carried his tray of sandwiches to his classroom and put them on a table with all the other food. The room looked jolly with paper chains hanging from the ceiling, cut out stars stuck to the windows and a crib in the corner with Jesus, Mary and Joseph made out of Plasticene; the children had done it all themselves.

Most of the day was spent playing games in the big hall while the teachers laid out the food ready for the party. At two-thirty it was to begin.

When Sam and his classmates got back they all gasped. It didn't look like their classroom anymore. Their little tables were covered with bright red paper and there were hats and streamers tucked in between the plates of food. And what food! Sandwiches, sausage rolls, crisps, cakes, jellies, biscuits and orange squash to drink.

"All right, children, dig in," yelled Mrs Peel, their teacher.

A big cheer went up and twenty or so little boys and girls 'dug in' to the feast.

Sam was pleased to see that everyone went for the sandwiches first. They liked the funny shapes. But then one little girl, who'd taken a bite from a heart shaped one, started coughing.

"Ugh! These are terrible. They've got bits in."

"Yuk! So has mine," said another.

Three or four more started to cough and splutter and Mrs Peel had to run round with the waste paper bin for them to spit out in. Sam felt that nasty tingle again.

Mrs Peel caught sight of his face. "Don't cry, dear," she begged. "Not now. We don't want to spoil the party."

Sam didn't cry. He was about to when the door was thrown open by the headmistress and in walked a very special visitor.

Mrs Peel curtsied. The visitor smiled and strolled around looking at the paintings and models and talking to some of the children as she went.

Stopping by Sam's table she pointed to his sandwiches.

"Those look nice. May I have one?" she asked.

Mrs Peel made a move to stop her but the visitor had already taken a bite. Everyone watched as she chewed, swallowed, frowned and then looked surprised. Mrs Peel picked up the waste paper bin, just in case.

The visitor opened her mouth . . . and spoke.

"Peanut butter?"

Sam nodded.

"Little white onions? Jam?"

Sam nodded again.

The very important visitor beamed. "My favourite sandwich filling. How did you know?"

The tingly feeling left Sam's tummy for once and for all. And after the visitor had gone, everyone wanted one of Sam's special sandwiches. But Sam politely said "no" and took them home to share with his dad for tea.

THE NIGHT BEFORE CHRISTMAS

Illustrated by Ken McKie.

'Twas the night before Christmas,
    when all through the house
Not a creature was stirring,
    not even a mouse;

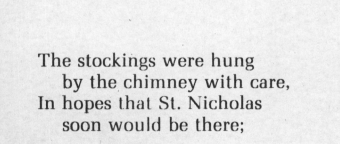

The stockings were hung
   by the chimney with care,
In hopes that St. Nicholas
   soon would be there;

The children were nestled
all snug in their beds,
While visions of sugar-plums
danced in their heads;

And Mamma in her kerchief, and I in my cap,
    Had just settled our brains for a long winter's nap;
When out on the lawn there arose such a clatter,
    I sprang from the bed to see what was the matter.

Away to the window I flew like a flash,
　　Tore open the shutters, and threw up the sash.
The moon on the breast of the new-fallen snow,
　　Gave the lustre of midday to objects below;
When, what to my wondering eyes should appear,
　　But a miniature sleigh and eight tiny reindeer,
With a little old driver, so lively and quick,
　　I knew in a moment, it must be St. Nick.

More rapid than eagles his coursers they came,
And he whistled, and shouted, and called them by name:
"Now, Dasher! now, Dancer! now, Prancer and Vixen!
On, Comet! on, Cupid! on, Donner and Blitzen!

To the top of the porch! to the top of the wall!
   Now dash away! dash away! dash away all!"
As dry leaves that before the wild hurricane fly,
   When they meet with an obstacle, mount to the sky,
So up to the house-top the coursers they flew,
   With the sleigh full of toys, and St. Nicholas too.
And then in a twinkle, I heard on the roof,
   The prancing and pawing, of each little hoof.

As I drew in my head, and was turning around,
  Down the chimney St. Nicholas came with a bound.
He was dressed all in fur, from his head to his foot,
  And his clothes were all tarnished with ashes and soot;
A bundle of toys he flung on his back,
  And he looked like a pedlar just opening his pack.

His eyes - how they twinkled! his dimples how merry!
   His cheeks were like roses, his nose like a cherry!
His droll little mouth was drawn like a bow,
   And the beard on his chin was as white as the snow;
The stump of a pipe he held tight in his teeth,
   And the smoke it encircled his head like a wreath;

He had a broad face and a little round belly,
   That shook when he laughed, like a bowlful of jelly.
He was chubby and plump - a right jolly old elf -
   And I laughed when I saw him, in spite of myself.
A wink in his eye and a twist of his head,

Soon gave me to know I had nothing to dread.
    He spoke not a word, but went straight to his work,
And filled all the stockings; then turned with a jerk,
    And laying his finger aside of his nose,
And giving a nod, up the chimney he rose;

He sprang to his sleigh,
    to his team gave a whistle,
And away they all flew
    like the down of a thistle.
But I heard him exclaim,
    ere he drove out of sight,
"Happy Christmas to all,
    and to all a good night!"

The Little Toy Theatre

"That!" exclaimed Mr. Penrose, pushing his chair away from the table and pulling out his napkin from under his chin, "was a perfectly splendid Christmas dinner."

His wife smiled. "Thank you, dear, but it's not over yet. There are tangerines and nuts to follow."

Mr. Penrose groaned. "If so much as a segment of orange or a tiny walnut passed my lips I'd burst all my buttons on my new waistcoat." And he puffed himself to show everyone what might happen, which the children, George, Elizabeth and Anne, found most amusing.

Mrs Penrose rang for the maid to come and clear away, then the family made its way into the parlour. Mr. Penrose promptly collapsed into his favourite armchair and the children set about playing with the presents they had opened that morning.

George emptied a box of shiny, red-uniformed, metal soldiers onto the floor and began setting them out. "Will you be the blue army, Father, so that I can have a battle?"

Mr. Penrose had been planning to have a quiet snooze, but he cheerfully lowered himself onto his knees and lined up the blue-coated opposition.

Elizabeth had been given a toy sewing machine for Christmas and was planning to make her dolls a new wardrobe of clothes.

"You will help me, won't you?" she begged her mother.

On hearing this, little Anne quickly looked up. "But you promised you'd help me," she whined. "You know I can't do it on my own, it's much too hard." Her present was a toy theatre made of card, complete with scenery, actors and a play to perform. Unfortunately for Anne, it all had to be cut out and stuck together before she could play with it.

"I know I said I'd help you," said her mother, "and so I shall, as soon as I've cut out something for Elizabeth to sew. Now be a good girl and bring me my workbox."

Slowly the little theatre began to take shape. George left the battle he was fighting to fix the stage together. Elizabeth put aside the party frock she was making for her best doll to help her sister cut out the characters and stick them to long strips of card with which they could be moved about. When it was finished, Anne was eager to put on a show.

"I think you ought to practise first," suggested her mother.

"Of course," said Anne. "But you don't practise - you rehearse."

George and Elizabeth wanted to join in. "Which play shall we do?" they asked.

"'Sleeping Beauty'," said Anne.

George groaned. "Why, there are hardly any fights or battles in 'Sleeping Beauty'."

"Good!" chorused the sisters. Then the threesome huddled together behind the sofa to rehearse.

After tea, Mr. and Mrs Penrose, Cook and Sarah, the maid, were called into the parlour and shown where to sit. Elizabeth played a little tune on the piano then joined her brother and sister behind a table on which was set a toy theatre. The curtain was about to go up.

Apart from some scenery getting stuck and one or two of the actors falling over, the first part of the play went well. First there was the christening, where the wicked fairy puts a curse on the baby Princess, followed by the sixteenth birthday party, where the Princess pricks her finger and falls asleep for a hundred years.

It was where the Prince meets a character called Ogre Frostytoes that things started to go wrong. George, who was doing their voices and moving them, thought that things needed livening up.

"Take that, you ugly ogre," said the Prince, jabbing the ogre with his sword.

"I'm not ugly," growled Ogre Frostytoes, jumping up and down on the Prince. None of it was in the script.

Anne was horrified. "Stop it," she cried. "Stop it at once. You're messing everything up. Oh, please tell him to stop, Father."

Mr. Penrose was trying not to laugh. "Now that's enough, George. If you're not careful you'll do some damage."

But it was too late. The little toy theatre had already begun to come apart. George saw what was happening and stopped.

"I am sorry, Anne," he said. "I didn't mean to do that. I can stick it together again. You'll see."

Anne wasn't listening. She had fled to the nursery in tears and, even though it was Christmas, that was where she stayed for the rest of the day.

When Anne opened her eyes the next morning the first thing she saw was the toy theatre sitting on the table at the end of her bed. George, who'd been waiting for her to wake up, popped his head round the door. "It's as good as new, Anne, I promise you. Er, you're not still cross with me, are you?" he asked, anxiously.

Anne gave a weak smile and tried to shake her head, but it hurt. Her throat hurt too and her eyes felt hot. George called his parents who hurried to the nursery.

"She has a slight temperature," said Mrs Penrose, "but I don't think we need call for the doctor. We'll keep her in bed today and see how she is tomorrow."

"What about tonight?" whispered Mr. Penrose. "What about the pantomime?" His wife shook her head and he gave a sigh. He had planned a surprise trip to see a real production of 'Sleeping Beauty' and he knew how disappointed Anne would be.

Anne was disappointed, but she tried not to show it when her brother and sister popped in to say goodnight before they left for the theatre. "It probably won't be half as good as my toy theatre," she joked. But when they had gone, she thought about them, dressed in their best clothes waiting for the thrilling moment when the curtain would rise and the play begin, and two tears trickled down her cheeks and plopped onto the eiderdown.

She dozed for a while and then something made her open her eyes and look at the little theatre. It seemed different, as though it was lit up and the Fairy Queen, who was standing in the centre of the stage, didn't look like a paper cut-out at all, she looked real. When she started to speak, Anne knew that she was.

"Quiet and still! Do not make a sound!
Wherever I am there is magic around.
A tale I will conjure of a King and a Queen,
Their daughter; a Princess, the loveliest ever seen.
Of good and of evil and a Prince, oh so bold!
So with no more ado, let our story unfold!"

And unfold it did. Anne watched her little cut-out players perform 'Sleeping Beauty' for her eyes alone. And finally, when the Prince woke the Princess with a kiss, Anne drifted off into a deep, peaceful sleep.

The next day Anne was feeling much better.

"I didn't miss the pantomime after all," she told her family. "The little people in my toy theatre came alive and did 'Sleeping Beauty' just for me."

"That's funny," said Mr. Penrose, "the people we saw in 'Sleeping Beauty' were just like the cardboard cut-outs."

George sniggered at his father's joke. "But it's true, Anne insisted. "When George put my theatre there yesterday, the Fairy Queen was alone on the stage, now there's the King and Queen and Sleeping Beauty and the Prince too."

"Perhaps you put them there and then forgot," suggested Elizabeth.

"No, I didn't," said Anne, starting to get tearful.

Mrs Penrose intervened. "If Anne said it happened, then it happened. We'll let her get some rest and perhaps she'll be well enough to come downstairs for lunch. There's cold turkey, Christmas pudding and trifle - your favourite."

When everyone had gone, Anne clambered to the bottom of her bed and picked up some of her cut-out characters. They seemed so lifeless in her hand that she was beginning to think she had dreamt it all. Then she noticed something glinting in a corner of the stage. She picked it up and a shiver of excitement ran through her whole body for she held between her fingers the tiniest of silver needles. It was much smaller than any in her mother's workbox and just like the one on which Sleeping Beauty pricked her finger in the play!

SANTA'S BEST COAT

It was Christmas Eve and the Head Gnome at the Gnometown Cleaners had just finished pressing Santa Claus's best red coat. "All those soot marks have come off," he said to the Smallest Gnome, as he brushed the white fur round the collar. "Now it looks as good as new."

The Head Gnome folded the coat carefully and put it in a large cardboard box. "Now take this along to Santa Claus right away," he told the Smallest Gnome.

So the Smallest Gnome set off, carrying the box carefully. He had quite a long way to go and the box seemed to get heavier and heavier and heavier. "Oh dear," sighed the Smallest Gnome, as he walked through Winter Wood. "I do wish I could have a rest for a few minutes."

Then he saw a large, hollow tree. "Just the place," he said to himself. "It will be sheltered from the wind in there." So he squeezed

GNOMETOWN CLEANERS

through the hole into the tree. Then he put down the box and sat on a pile of dry leaves.

The Smallest Gnome only meant to rest for a little while, but soon he felt very drowsy and fell asleep.

Much higher in the tree lived Sammy Squirrel and he was curled up on his bed of dry leaves. Suddenly he began to shiver. "It's getting much colder," said Sammy. "I really need some more

bedclothes."

So he jumped out of bed and looked out of his front door. "Goodness, it's beginning to snow," he cried. "I had better go and get some more dry leaves."

Sammy scurried down the tree trunk and hopped through the hole at the bottom. There he saw the Smallest Gnome, fast asleep. "Someone else is using my bedclothes," sighed Sammy. "What shall I do?"

Then he saw the box which the Smallest Gnome had put on the ground. He lifted the lid and saw Santa's best red coat. "This will be much warmer than leaves," chuckled Sammy, and he slipped in between the folds of the coat and pulled the lid back over him.

After a while the Smallest Gnome woke up. "Oh dear, it's getting dark," he gasped. "I shall have to hurry or Santa won't have his best red coat back in time to

GNOME TOWN CLEANERS

wear it tonight.

He looked out of the hollow tree and saw the snow, which was getting really deep. Then he saw something moving through the wood towards him.

It was Rudolph, Santa's reindeer. "Santa sent me to fetch his best red coat," called Rudolph. "He's been waiting for it all afternoon. Where have you been?"

"I fell asleep," confessed the Smallest Gnome."

"Dear me," said Rudolph, shaking his head. "You'd better ride on my back or Santa will be late starting tonight."

So the Smallest Gnome lifted the box onto Rudolph's back. "It's heavier than ever," he puffed, not knowing that Sammy Squirrel was curled up inside.

Off they trotted, through the wood, until at last they saw the lights shining through the windows of Santa's house. Santa himself was waiting by the open door, in his

waiting by the open door, in his shirtsleeves. "Have you cleaned my coat well?" he asked.

"Oh, yes," replied the Smallest Gnome, putting the box on the table and opening the lid.

"Goodness me, whoever is this?" cried Santa. Sammy Squirrel lay curled up on the coat, still fast asleep.

"Wake up!" called Santa. "We'll have to take you back to the wood."

So Santa put on his best red coat, and Sammy and the Smallest Gnome climbed on the sledge with him. First, Santa took Sammy Squirrel back to his tree house in Winter Wood and gave him a cosy quilt from a doll's bed to keep him warm.

"Oh, thank you," murmured Sammy, sleepily. "This will keep me warm for the rest of the winter."

Then Santa took the Smallest Gnome back to Gnometown and pulled a big parcel from the back of the sledge. "Perhaps this will help you to make your deliveries on time," he chuckled, as he drove away with Rudolph pulling his sledge over the snow.

"Thank you," called the Smallest Gnome, waving until they were out of sight. Then he quickly pulled all the wrappings off the big parcel.

Inside was a shiny new bicycle with a big carrier basket on the front. "It's just what I wanted!" cried the Smallest Gnome, jumping on and pedalling round and round with excitement. "This will make my work much easier."

So now the Smallest Gnome can make his deliveries at top speed, and Santa never has any trouble getting his best red coat back from the cleaners.

The King Who

Long ago in a far off country there lived a king who ruled fairly and wisely and seldom took a day off. He always worked very hard and expected his subjects to do the same.

His father, who had ruled before him, had been a lazy king who spent the time enjoying himself. He was always throwing parties and going on holiday and used any excuse to take a day off.

"That pimple on my nose seems to have disappeared," he would say to his wife. "I think I'll declare a national holiday in its honour." And from then on that day would be known as 'Passing of the Pimple Day'.

There was also 'Toenail Trimming Tuesday', 'Dog Bathing Day' and 'Fish Paste Friday', which was a bit like 'Pancake Day'.

There were so many holidays that very little work got done. No crops grew, no houses were built and children hardly ever went to school. The country got poorer and poorer, people went hungry and boys and girls grew up not knowing their ABC.

When the King died, his son came to power and everything changed. He abolished most of the silly holidays introduced by his father; which, at first, wasn't popular with his subjects for they had grown lazy and workshy. But when they saw the new king digging in the fields, sawing wood and hammering in nails, they followed his example and began to work had too.

Gradually the country grew rich again. But, although he could afford to take things easy, the King worked harder than ever.

Cancelled Christmas

"Please turn down the lamps and let us go to sleep," begged the Queen. "It's way past midnight."

The King was sitting up in bed polishing his riding boots.

"And why are you cleaning those? You never go riding."

"No, dear. Riding's a complete waste of time and energy. I've much more important things to do like weeding the flower beds and cutting the lawns." The King gazed around the room. "Would you like me to shine your dancing shoes while I'm at it?"

"What on earth for?" snapped the Queen. "I never go dancing. When was the last time we gave a ball or a party? We don't even celebrate my birthday anymore," she said, sadly.

The King gave a grin. "So that's why you never look any older. Er . . would you mind moving your head so I can polish those bed knobs."

His wife let out a scream of exasperation and threw a pillow at him.

It was Autumn and the Queen was looking forward to Christmas. It was one of the few holidays left. She was discussing all the arrangements with the Chancellor when the King rushed in clutching a calendar. She was immediately filled with dread.

"I've thought how we can fit more working days into the year," he exclaimed, pleased with himself.

"What do we want with more working days?" asked the Queen, "haven't we enough already?"

"No, my dear, there are never enough. Why, there's that order for eight hundred milking stools for the King of Lagunia and six hundred christening spoons for the . . ."

"All right, all right," said the Queen impatiently. "What are you getting rid of this time, 'Pudding Mixing Day', 'Present Wrapping Wednesday' or 'Snowman Sunday'?"

"Christmas Day!" announced the King, proudly.

"Christmas Day!" echoed the Queen, horrified. "But you can't. I'm making plans."

"Exactly," said the King. "If I get rid of Christmas all those other days go too. They won't be necessary." He turned to the Chancellor. "Put out a decree at once that this year Christmas will be cancelled."

"Oh will it?" thought the Queen. "We'll see about that."

His subjects weren't very pleased with the news, but they simply grumbled amongst themselves and hoped the King would change his mind. He didn't.

The night before Christmas Eve, the Queen lay awake waiting for

her husband to fall asleep. Then, as soon as she heard midnight chime, she slipped out of bed and crept round the castle changing the date on all the calendars. Instead of reading December 24th, she had put them forward a day to December 25th - Christmas Day. Then she went back to bed to wait for morning.

"Would you believe it it's Christ . . . er, December 25th already," said the King. "Doesn't time fly?

Well I'd better be off. Got to clear the snow off the castle drawbridge. There weren't any presents, I mean parcels left for me, were there?"

The Queen shook her head and the King left, looking disappointed.

It was lunchtime when they met again, seated either end of the long banqueting table.

"It does look gloomy in here," commented the King. "Don't you think a few decorations might brighten it up a bit?"

"They might," said the Queen, "but with everyone working it hardly seems worth doing. Ah, lunch."

A servant placed before them plates of bread and cheese. The King's face fell. "No turkey? No stuffing? No cranberry sauce?"

"No dear," answered the Queen. "This is an everyday working lunch."

The King spent a cold afternoon breaking the ice on the castle horse troughs. When he came in at tea time he was looking forward to a slice of iced fruit cake, but all he got was bread and dripping.

"I don't suppose there's a mince pie or two lying around," he asked.

"Oh no," the Queen told him. "I only make those at Christmas."

The King looked thoroughly miserable.

"I think I may have made a terrible mistake, cancelling Christmas," he sighed. "I miss the presents, the decorations, the food and the fun. Tomorrow I shall put it back on the calendar. What a pity we'll have to wait a whole year to enjoy it."

The Queen decided that he had learned his lesson and it was time to tell him about the trick she had played. ". . . . . . . and so you see, dear, it's still only Christmas Eve," she explained.

The King gave a whoop of joy and sent out messengers to tell his subjects that tomorrow was a holiday and that they should stop work and prepare for Christmas Day.

And when the Queen's birthday came round, he threw the biggest party that the castle had ever seen.

The North Wind

The North Wind whistles through the street
And swirls the dust around our feet;
It stings our faces when we meet
A gust of snow or icy sleet.

It scutters round the Market Place
Among the stalls of fruit and lace,
And tugs each cover from its base
As owners to the rescue race;

And as their goods blow all about
We hear the chestnut seller shout;
On this cold day there is no doubt
His chestnuts hot will soon sell out.

And while we're crowding round to buy
We see the bags and papers fly;
A big balloon goes whirling high -
The wind has tossed it to the sky.

Our shopping finished, cheeks aglow,
We battle through the North Wind's blow;
With streaming scarves and heads bent low
It's very gladly home we go.

THE NUTCRACKER

Re-told by Anne McKie. Illustrated by Ken McKie.

This enchanting tale took place
almost a century ago. It is a story full
of fantasy and perhaps a little magic.
You may think it was all just a dream
or did it really happen?

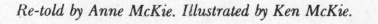

Every Christmas Eve, Mayor Stahlbaum
gave a grand party for his son and
daughter and all their young friends.

Now Mayor Stahlbaum was a very rich man, and young Fritz and Clara had a huge nursery full of expensive and unusual toys.

Clara had so many different dolls - she couldn't remember all their names. While her brother Fritz had too many soldiers to count! These soldiers were kept in a model fort twice as high as Fritz himself!

At last it was Christmas Eve and the party was in full swing. Clara and Fritz and their young guests eagerly unwrapped the presents that lay beneath the sparkling Christmas tree.

What fun it was. The children joined in all the games and dancing. They made so much noise the grown-ups felt quite tired out.

This Christmas Eve, the old man had brought a very special present for Clara. It was a Nutcracker doll in the shape of a soldier.

"This is my favourite Christmas present of all!" cried Clara with delight. "Isn't my Nutcracker handsome?" and she held up her doll for all to see.

"I think he's the ugliest thing I ever saw!" shouted Clara's brother. It was getting late and young Fritz was tired (and had eaten far too many sweets.)

"Give it to me!" he whined. Quick as a flash Fritz grabbed the Nutcracker, pushed a huge hazelnut into its mouth and jammed it shut.

There was a loud crack and the doll's head was split. The nut rolled out and Fritz flung the Nutcracker onto the floor in temper.

Near to tears, Clara picked up her broken Nutcracker. But Herr Drosselmeyer gently tied his handkerchief round the doll's head and whispered, "In the morning it will be handsome once more!"

Late that night, when all the house was asleep, Clara crept down to the nursery.

As the clock struck midnight, Clara glanced up and was very startled to see Herr Drosselmeyer sitting right on the very top.

What a fright Clara got. Far across the floor, from every corner of her nursery, swarms of mice came scampering towards her!

Clara sprang backwards, for the mice looked as big as herself - and so did the soldiers.

As the little girl let out a scream of fright, the soldiers came to life. They blew their bugles and banged their drums and were soon fighting a fierce battle against the mice.

Then Clara gasped in amazement as her Nutcracker doll jumped out of his box as if by magic. He grabbed the nearest sword and joined the soldiers in battle.

All of a sudden from the depth of the army of mice, sprang the evil Mouse King. He had a golden crown on his head and was waving a great sharp sword.

It was quite clear that the mice were winning. There were so many of them.

As the Mouse King came towards the Nutcracker with his sharp sword, Clara pulled off her shoe and aimed it at his head. The shoe caught the Mouse King off guard and he fell to the ground.

In a trice, all the mice vanished, and standing in the Nutcracker's place - was a handsome prince!

"Come with me, Clara!" said the Nutcracker Prince, "and I will take you to a wonderful land!"

Without another word, he whisked Clara off through the wondrous Kingdom of Snow, where the little snowflakes danced in and out of the glittering trees.

The Nutcracker Prince had Clara by the hand and soon they came to the marvellous Land of Sweets, and there at the palace to greet them was the Sugar Plum Fairy.

"Clara saved me from the wicked Mouse King!" the Prince smiled as he told the Fairy about their battle with the mice.

"You must be a very brave girl!" the Sugar Plum Fairy told Clara. "Sit here in the place of honour and receive our grateful thanks."

With that she led Clara to a marzipan throne next to the Prince, clapped her hands and cried, "Let the celebrations begin!"

First came dancers from Spain and from Arabia - Clara
was enchanted.

Next came acrobats from China and swirling, stamping Cossacks from Russia - Clara was spellbound.

Last of all came the twirling, whirling Flower Dolls that waltzed with the Sugar Plum Fairy - Clara was lost in a world of fantasy.

Then everyone in the Land of Sweets began to wave goodbye, and Clara felt herself floating on a big soft cloud, just like a dream.

Very gently she drifted far away until the Sugar Plum Fairy and the Nutcracker Prince slowly faded, and the magical Land of Sweets was left far behind.

The next thing Clara knew, she was lying on the nursery floor back in her own house, and held tightly in her arms was her Nutcracker doll.

The little girl realised it was morning. Had it all been just a lovely dream?

Clara ran to the nursery window. As she looked out that cold Christmas Day, she could just make out the dark figure of Herr Drosselmeyer disappearing down the street in the softly falling snow...

Santa's Ride

"Christmas is coming!"
    A whisper had stirred
Mice in the meadow.
    A half-awake bird
Peeped from its shelter
    where berries hung bright,
Saw the moon rising
    to shed her pale light
Over the country
    and over the town
Where, through the day,
    the soft snow drifting down
Covered the land;
    now a mantle of white
Sparkled with frost
    in the hush of the night.

Stockings were hung
    at the foot of each bed,
Waiting for Santa
    to come with his sled;
Each sleepy head
    to its pillow had flown:
"Christmas is coming!"
    the whisper had grown.
Louder it blew
    over sea, over shore,
Santa could hear it
    and lingered no more:
"Away now, my beauties,"
    he called to his deer,
Climbing his sledge
    with its load of good cheer.

"Christmas is coming!"
　　the waves of the sea
Echoed the bells
　　as they rang merrily;
Mice in the meadow
　　saw Santa pass by,
Birds sang their greetings
　　that reached to the sky.
Santa heard all
　　as he made his long ride,
Stars for his lanterns,
　　the moon for his guide
Lighting his way
　　to each cottage and house,
Silent as snowfall,
　　as soft as a mouse.

Letters to Santa
　　had asked him to bring
Cycles and spaceships,
　　a doll that can sing;
Here a small cradle
　　and there a big train,
Toy bears and tea sets,
　　a car or a plane.
Nothing, it seemed,
　　was too large or too small;
Santa, at last,
　　had delivered them all.
Nobody spied him,
　　so fast had he sped,
Leaving his toys
　　at the foot of each bed.

Only the mice
in the meadow had seen,
Only the birds
in the holly bush green;
When the young dreamers
with morning awoke,
Giving their stockings
a prod or a poke.

Quickly they tumbled
from bed to the floor
Wide-eyed with wonder
at toys in galore.
Then they all shouted
and gave a big cheer:
"Hooray for Santa,
now Christmas is here!"

A Picture
To Paint

The Nativity Play

"Please, Miss! Joseph's supposed to come with me, not the three Wise Men," complained the Virgin Mary.

"Yes, Cathy, I know," said the teacher wearily. But you musn't stop every time some little thing goes wrong. Haven't you heard the saying 'the show must go on'?"

From the blank look on Cathy's face it was evident that she hadn't.

"It means," Mrs Peel went on, "that whatever happens don't stop, keep going if the scenery falls down, or your costume falls down or the actor falls down. Now, let's start again, and please try to get it right."

Mrs Peel nodded to the piano and for the umpteenth time that afternoon Mrs Graham played the opening bars to 'Once In Royal David's City'.

Inglenook Infants were rehearsing their nativity play. The school was famous for it. It was put on every year, all the parents came to see it and it usually went very well, but this year nothing seemed to be going right.

Mrs Peel had never done the nativity before. It had always been left to Mrs Morris to organise, but she had retired that summer and the headmistress had asked Mrs Peel to take on the task. "I'm sure you'll make a wonderful job of it," the head had said.

Mrs Peel had thought so too at the time, but now she wasn't so sure. Joseph couldn't remember where he was supposed to stand, the Wise Men kept fidgeting and the Shepherds giggled all the time.

The school bell rang out; it was going home time.

"Please, Miss. Can my auntie come and see the play as well as my mum and dad?" asked Pearl Wilson.

"I expect so," sighed Mrs Peel, although she couldn't imagine why Pearl's auntie or anyone would want to sit through this shambles of a Christmas story.

The next morning there was more rehearsing; this time in costume and on the stage in the big hall.

Someone's mum who kept horses had provided bales of straw to dot about the stage. Mr. Green, the school caretaker, had built a stable and a manger and hung up a large star which, when it worked, lit up. It all looked marvellous and Mrs Peel hoped that once the children put on costumes and got amongst the scenery that it would all come right.

Once again the piano struck up with 'Once In Royal David's City. . .' and Joseph stepped on the hem of Mary's robe so she couldn't move.

"Please, Miss!"

"Keep going, Cathy, keep going," Mrs Peel urged.

This time everyone got onto the stage, but the Wise Men kept staring into the hall forgetting to sing and one of the Shepherds was making rude noises to make others laugh.

"Sam Stevens, stop giggling," she called, trying not to lose her patience. "And hold your lamb the right way round."

That made him giggle all the more.

They hadn't even managed a complete run through when the dinner bell sounded. The performance was to be that afternoon.

Those in the play were allowed to stay in costume and eat a packed lunch up on the stage while the other infants had their dinners on the long tables down on the hall floor. It made the cast feel really important.

Alan, one of the Wise Men, started to show off while 'Miss' wasn't looking. He threw a piece of cheese and pickle sandwich at a Shepherd but it missed and fell into the manger where it had stayed.

After lunch, the tables were cleared away and the benches were turned to face the stage. It wasn't long before parents started to arrive and take their seats for the show.

In a nearby classroom the cast waited for their cue to begin.

"Now, please, dears, sing your words clearly, try not to step on each other's clothes and don't gaze around the room," Mrs Peel told them. "It's the baby Jesus you should be looking at not someone's auntie in the front row." The children giggled, nervously.

"Good luck," she added, as the familiar strains of 'Once In Royal David's City' rang out.

Singing sweetly, they filed onto the stage. First Joseph and then Mary, who laid the baby Jesus in the manger. As she did so she gave a small gasp and Mrs Peel, who was watching from the side of the stage, thought that something had gone wrong and that Cathy was going to stop. But, to her great relief, Cathy did as she'd been told and kept singing and staring wide-eyed into the manger.

As Joseph, the Wise Men and the Shepherds gathered round, they too could see what had made Cathy gasp. It was a little brown mouse sitting in the straw, nibbling a piece of cheese and pickle sandwich which Alan had thrown at lunchtime. It didn't seem the least bit worried about the singing or the presence of a large china doll.

With eyes glued to the munching mouse, the children sang their way through 'The Holly and The Ivy', 'The First Noel' and 'O Come All Ye Faithful', which everyone joined in.

Mrs Peel was delighted. They looked a picture grouped round the manger gazing down at the baby Jesus. It was really quite moving. One or two of the mums were having to dab their eyes with handkerchiefs.

When it was over the children dashed back on stage to look in the manger, but the mouse had gone.

"So that's why none of you could take your eyes off the manger," said Mrs Peel, after Cathy had told her about the mouse.

"It must have come out of one of those bales of straw," said one of the boys, pointing.

Mrs Peel shivered. "Well I hope it's gone back there." She wasn't too keen on mice.

The headmistress tapped her on the shoulder. "Well done, Mrs Peel. A perfectly splendid nativity." Then she lowered her voice. "This year's infants can be a bit of a handful at times. But there they were today, standing round the manger looking just like little angels. I don't know how you did it!"

And Mrs Peel wasn't about to tell her that the success of that year's nativity was entirely due to a little brown mouse and a piece of cheese and pickle sandwich.

The No Snowman

"Roses still blooming in December, whoever heard of such a thing?"
exclaimed Granny Bates, looking out into the garden. "When I was a girl
I'd have been out there building a snowman by now."

"I can remember it snowing once," said her grandson, Joe, "but it all
melted before I could go out and play in it," he added, sadly.

His younger sister, Polly, climbed onto her grandma's lap. "Tell me
about the snowman, Granny," she begged.

"Oh, there were lots of them," she explained. "Me and my brother would
make one each winter it snowed. But there was one in particular that I
remember. It stayed in the garden for days and days and then, when it
began to thaw, it melted ever so slowly until it was a tiny snowball in the
middle of the grass."

"I want to make a snowman like that," said Polly. "I want to make it now."

"Well you can't," her brother told her, "there's no snow." Being a few years older than his sister he was much more practical.

Mr. Bates walked in and Polly jumped off her grandma's lap and rushed up to him. "I want to make a snowman, Daddy. Please can I? Oh, please, please!"

"That might be rather difficult, seeing as how there's no snow about," he laughed.

"That's what I said," chipped in Joe.

Mr. Bates scratched his head and thought for a moment. "Tell you what, why don't you make a No-Snowman instead?"

Polly thought it was a wonderful idea, but Joe was more cautious.

"How do we make a No-Snowman?" he asked.

"Wait until tomorrow and you'll see," was all their father would say.

The next day, wearing their warmest clothes, for it had turned quite cold, Polly and Joe joined their father in the garden. He had been rummaging in his tool shed and had brought out a couple of old sacks, one big, one small. He proceeded to fill them up with all sorts of garden rubbish until they were two fat shapes. Then Mr. Bates stuck the small one on top of the big one so that it vaguely looked like a head on a body.

"There, that's my work done. It's up to you to finish him off," he told them and went indoors.

Polly and Joe looked first at the oddly shaped sacks and then at each other.

"What shall we do now?" said Polly.

"I don't know," answered Joe, grumpily. "Whoever heard of a No-Snowman any way? I'm going in."

"No!" cried Polly, grabbing at his coat. "You're to stay and help me, Daddy said."

"No he didn't. Now let me go."

"No!" screamed his sister, holding on tight.

Joe yanked his coat out of Polly's hands and she sat down on the ground with a bump. "I'm going to tell Mummy you pushed me," she said, scrambling up.

"Hello, you two," said a neighbour, popping her head over the fence. "What's that you've got there?"

"It's a No-Snowman," mumbled Joe, rather embarrassed.

"A No-Snowman? That's a clever idea. Hang on, I think I've got something he can wear." She disappeared and returned carrying an old overcoat which she passed over the fence.

"Thanks," said Polly and Joe, as they draped the coat around the sack and did up the buttons. It was a perfect fit.

Their grandma suddenly appeared with a pair of woollen gloves which they tucked up into the sleeves. The No-Snowman now had hands. Polly and Joe stood back to look at him. From behind they heard a giggle. They were being watched by some children from down the road.

"What's that?" they called.

"It's a funny kind of scarecrow," joked one.

"Bit late for Guy Fawkes night," jeered another.

Joe didn't know what to say. These were the people he went to school with and he knew they'd make fun of him if he told them what it really was.

Then Polly spoke. "Actually, it's a No-Snowman," she said in a rather grand voice.

There was a silence, then a boy shouted, "A No-Snowman, what a great idea. Can we help?" And without waiting for a reply they rushed off, shortly to return with scarves, hats, an umbrella and even a pair of boots for the funny sack man.

They were a noisy crowd and soon the garden was filled with shouting and laughing as they argued about which scarf looked best and how he should wear his hat.

"I like making a No-Snowman," yelled Polly.

A cheer went up as Mrs Bates arrived with a tray of hot chocolate and biscuits, but it was quickly followed with a groan when she pointed out that the No-Snowman hadn't got a face. No-one could think of how to make him one.

"Buttons!" cried Polly and Joe's mother, as she dashed into the house and came out with her sewing box and some strong glue. She stuck on two blue buttons for the eyes, a pink button for the nose and four red ones for the mouth. She made him look as though he was smiling.

"Now he's finished what are you going to call him?"

The children got into a huge argument over his name and Polly's voice could be heard above the rest, crying, "But he's my No-Snowman, so I should choose the name."

Then everyone went quiet when something most unexpected happened. It started to snow, slowly at first and then thick and fast until it covered the ground.

The children from down the road stamped and yelled. "We're off to make a proper snowman. We don't want your silly No-Snowman anymore." And away they went, taking their scraves and hats and all the other things they'd brought.

Polly and Joe suddenly felt cold and went inside.

That afternoon the children from down the road built their snowman. Polly and Joe could see it from the upstairs window.

"We could go out and make one too, if you like," offered Joe.

Polly shook her head. "No thanks. I think I like our No-Snowman best."

"So do I," agreed Joe. "And at least he'll still be there when it's thawed. He'll last for even longer than the one Granny made."

The words had barely left Joe's lips than the sun came out and shone warmly. In no time at all the thick blanket had become a few snowy patches and the 'proper' snowman was just a little white pile.

The No-Snowman still stood proud and smiling in the corner of the garden and while other winters and other snowmen came and went, he stayed there for a long, long time.

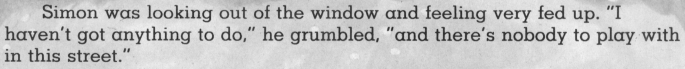

Simon was looking out of the window and feeling very fed up. "I haven't got anything to do," he grumbled, "and there's nobody to play with in this street."

"Look, it's starting to snow," said his mother. "When it's deep enough you can go outside and make a snowman."

Simon watched the snow falling faster and faster. It got deeper and deeper, until Simon shouted: "There's plenty of snow to make a snowman. Hooray!"

Simon's mother helped him put on his coat and boots, then grabbing his warm gloves, he ran outside to play in the snow.

First he piled up the snow with a spade, to make the snowman's body,

then he rolled a great big snowball for his head. "How can I make his face?" he shouted to his mother, who was watching through the window.

In a few minutes she came out with two bottle tops for his eyes, a carrot for his nose and a piece of orange peel cut in a half-circle for his mouth. "What are you going to call him?" she asked.

"I'll call him Smiley Snowman," said Simon, "because he looks so happy."

Then Simon went indoors to have his tea and Smiley Snowman stayed outside. It began to get dark and all the street lights came on. "I wish I'd got someone to talk to," said Smiley, "but I can't see another snowman anywhere along this street."

Before Simon went to bed he took a last peep out of his bedroom window and said: "There's Smiley Snowman. I'll play with him again tomorrow."

But when Simon had gone to sleep, Smiley Snowman said: "I'm tired of staying out here all on my own. I'll go along the street and see if I can find someone to play with."

Smiley went down the garden path, opened the gate and began to move along the street with a funny, shuffling walk. But not one other snowman could he find, because Simon was the only boy in the whole street and the grown-ups hadn't made any snowmen to play with.

Smiley shuffled on through the town. By this time everybody else had gone to bed , so there was no-one to stop him.

At last Smiley reached the children's playground. He stopped and listened. He could hear a funny, squeaking noise. It was coming from one

of the swings.

There, at last, was another snowman! He was swinging to and fro, all on his own, looking very sad. But when he saw Smiley, he started to smile back. He jumped off the swing and called: "Do come and play on the see-saw!"

The other snowman's name was Toby Topper, because he was wearing an old top hat. He and Smiley had a lot of fun together in the playground. First they see-sawed up and down, then they whirled round and round on the roundabout. Then they tried the big slide.

"Whee, this is fun!" laughed Smiley. "I'm going to do that again."

Very soon they both started to feel very warm. As snowmen don't like to get hot, they found some long icicles and licked them like iced lollies.

"It is fun to have someone to play with," said Toby Topper. "I don't like being left here all by myself."

"Come home with me," said Smiley. "I'm sure Simon won't mind."

By the time they got back to Simon's garden the sun was just beginning to rise. Simon woke up and looked out of his window and saw *two* snowmen there. He couldn't believe his eyes.

He called his mother to come and see them, and she was very surprised. "I wonder how ever the other snowman go there?" she cried.

Then, after breakfast, some boys and girls came knocking at the door. "Can we have our snowman back?" they said. "We made him in the playground yesterday. We know he's our snowman because he's wearing a top hat, but we don't know how he got into your garden!"

They tried to move Toby Topper but he just would not budge. "It's no good, you'll have to stay and play with him in my garden," said Simon, by now getting quite excited.

So they all played with Smiley and Toby Topper until the sun grew so warm, both snowmen began to feel very uncomfortable.

Then Simon's mother called everyone else indoors to have some orange juice and biscuits.

Smiley looked at Toby and Toby looked at Smiley. "I think it's time we went off to Snowmanland," they both said.

When Simon and his friends came back into the garden, Smiley and Toby Topper had disappeared. All they left behind was an old top hat lying on the ground.

Nobody found out where the snowmen had gone, but after that Simon always had lots of friends to play with.

THE LITTLE FIR TREE

Re-told by Anne McKie. Illustrated by Ken McKie.

Once upon a time, in a clearing deep in the middle of a great forest, there grew a Little Fir Tree.

All around him were giant pine trees with long straight trunks, their top branches almost reaching the sky - well at least, that's how it looked to the Little Fir Tree, who longed to grow tall and tower over the whole forest.

The animals who lived nearby loved the Little Fir Tree. In spring and summer they played all day beneath his soft feathery branches. Small birds built their nests amongst his sweet smelling needles, sheltered from the strong winds that swept through the giant pines high above.

All day long, the Little Fir Tree could hear the sound of axes ringing through the forest, as the woodcutters felled the tallest trees and brought them crashing to the ground.

The Little Fir Tree sighed to himself: "I wish my trunk was tall and straight enough to be a ship's mast, or even the strongest beam in a big house!"

With that, he stretched his small branches as hard as he could, to try and make himself grow a bit bigger.

One day, the wind that swayed the Little Fir Tree's branches began to grow colder and the first few snowflakes of winter started to fall.

The animals all disappeared for their long winter sleep, and most of the birds had flown away to summer lands. Very soon the snow lay thick on the ground - even the woodcutters had left the forest until next spring.

Was the Little Fir Tree lonely? Oh, no! For soon new exciting sounds began to fill the air. It was the laughter and shrieks of happy children, as they tobogganed down the forest's snowy slopes.

All of a sudden the Little Fir Tree was surrounded by three delighted children. They danced around him in the snow, clapping and singing. "We've found the most beautiful tree in the forest," they chorused.

The Little Fir Tree, his branches sparkling and twinkling with frost, almost blushed with pride.

"Father! Come quickly!" all three cried together. "Here is our Christmas Tree!"

Before he knew what was happening, the Little Fir Tree
had been cut down and gently placed on a sledge. Very
soon he was speeding along between the great trunks of
the giant pines, until the forest was left far behind.

Everyone seemed so delighted with the Little Fir Tree
that he felt happy too.

At last they came to the small town at the foot of the forest's slopes.

As the children ran through the streets, they shouted to everybody they met, "Look at our tree! Isn't it the most perfect Christmas Tree you ever saw?"

The Little Fir Tree felt rather puzzled. "What on earth is a Christmas Tree?" he thought to himself.

The Little Fir Tree was beginning to enjoy himself. "This is much better than becoming one of those giant pine trees and living all your life in the forest."

"Where did you get that lovely little tree?" "Is he for sale?" "Please can I buy him?" people shouted as they passed by. The three children just grinned and shook their heads.

All at once, the Little Fir Tree looked around. He saw fir trees everywhere! They were standing in windows, outside front doors, on porches and in gardens.

"These must be Christmas Trees!" smiled the Little Fir Tree, feeling proud. "Then I shall be the very best Christmas Tree of all!"

When the Little Fir Tree reached the children's house,
he was carefully carried inside and placed upright in a tub.
That night, the whole family gathered round to decorate
their Christmas Tree - for it was Christmas Eve.

Everyone helped to hang the decorations on the Little
Fir Tree's branches. Soon this very special little tree was
covered with toys and fruit, cookies and candy, and lots of
tiny candles. And at the very top - a golden star!

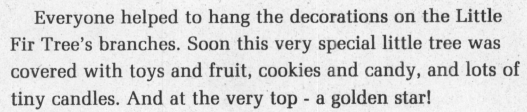

There stood the Little Fir Tree quivering with pride. He really was the Most Beautiful Christmas Tree in the World!

The tiny candles twinkled like a thousand stars and filled the room with their sparkling light. The Little Fir Tree shone in all his glory, for it was Christmas Eve - the most magical night of the year.

Before they went to bed on this very special night, the children left their stockings beneath the Little Fir Tree. "No one has ever seen Father Christmas," whispered the children, very excited, "and he won't come until everyone is fast asleep."

But late that night Father Christmas did come. He slipped silently into the room, quietly took the children's presents from his sack and popped them underneath the tree.

Just for a moment he stepped back to admire the beautiful Little Fir Tree. He gave a broad smile, a twinkle of his eye, then vanished up the chimney.

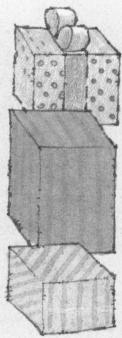

The Little Fir Tree felt so happy to be a Christmas Tree, and very proud that he alone had really seen Father Christmas.

During the twelve days of Christmas, the Little Fir Tree had a wonderful time. Many visitors called at the house to admire him, and lots of children came in from the street to see how beautiful he looked. The Little Fir Tree loved every moment of it, and thought it would last for ever.

All too soon Twelfth Night came, which marked the end of Christmas.

Every single decoration in the house was taken down and packed away until next year.

The Little Fir Tree looked so bare. Lots of his needles had dropped onto the floor and his branches were brittle and dry. Worse was to come! Along with all the other old greenery in the house, the poor Little Fir Tree was taken outside and burned on the bonfire.

And that was the end of the Little Fir Tree!

The whole family felt sorry that Christmas was over and that their lovely tree had met such a sad end. So there and then, the children's father made a promise that it would not happen again.

During the long cold months of winter that followed, the family never forgot their Little Fir Tree. The children remembered his dazzling brilliance, and it made them feel happy through the dark winter nights.

Spring came at last! The warm sun melted the snow and ice and the forest came to life once more.

One bright sunny morning, Father took the three
children to the spot where he had cut down the Little Fir
Tree.

This time he took with him a spade and not an axe.
Together they carefully dug up three trees - one for each of
the children; a tiny tree, a middle size tree and one a bit **bigger**.

Back home they planted the biggest tree in the garden, the middle size one near the house, and the tiny tree in a pot near the door.

So when next Christmas came they would have fir trees that would keep growing, and not have to be thrown out and burned like the poor Little Fir Tree!

As the years went by, the children decorated their trees every Christmas. On the two outside, they tied hundreds of glistening lamps. The smallest tree was carried inside every year until it grew too big for the house.

Now the children have grown up and have children of their own - and grandchildren. The three fir trees have grown, and now they are the tallest in the valley. And every Christmas Eve, they shine so brightly, for all the world to see.

The Dog Who Fetched Father Christmas

Mr. and Mrs Banks, their son, Matthew, and his little dog, Teddy, were on their way to spend Christmas on the farm with Matt's grandparents.

Teddy loved riding in the car. He would pad up and down on the back seat, first looking out of one side of the car and then the other. Mr. and Mrs Banks sat in the front singing 'The Twelve Days of Christmas'. Everyone was in a jolly mood, except Matt.

"Come on, Matt, why don't you join in?" said his mother. But Matt stayed silent.

Teddy stopped padding up and down and looked at his master. Something was wrong. He had never seen him look so glum.

"Cheer up," said his father. "After all it is Christmas."

"Then why can't we have it at home?"

Mr. and Mrs Banks were astonished to hear what their son had said. "I don't understand," said his mother, "when we told you we were spending Christmas at the farm you were thrilled and couldn't wait for the holiday to come."

Matt mumbled something about Father Christmas.

"What about Father Christmas?" asked his mother.

"How will he know where I am?"

His parents looked puzzled. Matt went on.

"How will he know where to leave my presents if I'm at the farm? When we wrote my letter telling him what I wanted for Christmas we put *our* address on it. He'll go to the house and if I'm not there he'll take my presents away again."

His parents smiled at each other. "Father Christmas will know where to find you, you can be sure of that," they told him.

But Matt wasn't convinced, and neither was Teddy.

When they arrived at the farm Matt cheered up a little. There were hugs and kisses from his grandparents then everyone tucked into a delicious farmhouse supper. Afterwards they played card games in front of a roaring fire until it was time for Matt to go to bed. He kissed everyone goodnight then headed for the door.

"Haven't you forgotten something?" said Granny. Matt stopped and frowned.

"Aren't you going to hang up your stocking ready for Father Christmas?" Matt shook his head.

His mother sighed. "He thinks that because he's not at home, Father Christmas won't know where to leave his presents."

"What nonsense," laughed Granny. "Of course Father Christmas will know where you are."

"That's what we told him," said Mr. Banks.

Half-heartedly, Matt helped Granny hang up his stocking - a large woolly sock with darns in the toe and heel - and then went to bed. Teddy went with him and settled down by Matt's feet. He listened to Matt sniffing back his tears before dropping off to sleep. Teddy stayed wide awake, thinking.

He thought how miserable Matt would be if he woke up in the morning with no presents to unwrap and play with and he decided to do something about it. He would go back to the house,

wait for the sleigh to come, and
then fetch Father Christmas to the
farm.

He slipped off the bed and went
downstairs. The grown-ups were
looking through an old photograph
album and didn't notice the little
dog make his way to the door. It
was shut tight. He hid behind a
curtain deciding what to do.

Just then Grandpa got up to go
out and check all the animals. He
put on his big coat and boots, said,
"Shan't be long", and opened the
door. Teddy scooted out between
Grandpa's legs leaving him
wondering whether he'd seen
something or not.

Over the fields he went in what he hoped was the direction of the motorway, but in the dark it all seemed different and strange. It was also starting to snow.

On and on he ran until his paws were sore. He was beginning to think he had chosen the wrong direction when, on reaching the top of a hill, he found himself gazing at the bright lights and the wide lanes of the motorway. He gave a bark of

He had a couple of goes, but each time he slithered back to the ground. Then he heard the engine start up. Teddy hurled himself into the air, cleared the tailboard and fell into the lorry just as it was moving off. Bruised but pleased with himself, Teddy settled down for the ride.

When the lorry slowed down, Teddy guessed that they had left the motorway and poked out his nose for a look around. The streets looked familiar so he decided to get off. He scrambled to the top of the tailboard, balanced there for a moment then leaped into the air, landing flat in the road. In the distance he heard the faint sound of jingling bells. He picked himself up and hurried on.

Turning a corner he could see Santa's sleigh hovering over his house. When he got there he could hear moving about inside so he scratched at the front door. There was no answer, so he scratched again. When that was ignored he barked, very loudly. The door was opened in a trice by a red-coated, white-bearded gentleman who seemed to be rather cross.

"What do you think you're doing?" he hissed. "I'll never deliver all these presents by morning if you wake everyone up."

Teddy took hold of his red coat and tried to pull him out the door.

"Wouldn't it be easier if you told me what you want. I can understand you, you know."

Teddy stopped tugging and started talking.

"I see," said Father Christmas, when Teddy had finished. "So, if your master's not here, where is he?"

"Wuff," wuffed Teddy. "Wuff, wuff, wuff. Wuff, wuff."

joy and slid down the snowy bank to the lay-by below.

A lorry was parked there and Teddy decided to get a lift. The back of the lorry was open but high up. He would have to jump.

"Then I'd better be off. By the way, would you like a lift?"

Teddy wagged his tail. He'd been wondering how he would get back to the farm. Tucked up under a warm rug on the seat of Santa's sleigh, he went fast asleep.

When he woke up he was surprised to find himself back at the bottom of Matt's bed. It was morning and Matt was still asleep.

"Wuff," barked Teddy. "Wuff, wuff." 'Time to get up, lazybones,' he was saying. 'Don't you know it's Christmas Day?'

"All right," said Matt, drowsily, "I'll get up. But I don't know why you're so excited. Father Christmas won't have been. I know it."

"I wouldn't be so sure of that." Matt's mother was standing in

the doorway, a big smile on her face.

Matt leaped out of bed and tore downstairs, Teddy at his heels. They nearly fell over each other getting into the sitting room.

Matt's stocking was bulging with toys, sweets, fruit and nuts and on the floor were several brightly wrapped parcels. Hanging next to Matt's stocking was another smaller one. Inside it was a rubber bone, a new collar and some doggy treats. How it had got there puzzled everyone except Matt and Teddy.

"Thank you, Father Christmas," yelled Matt.

"Wuff, wuff, wuff, wuff," went Teddy, which meant exactly the same thing.

Snow For Christmas

Tony and Carol had been to the village shop to buy some Christmas decorations. Now they were on their way home along Holly Lane. Carol kept stopping to peep at the paper chains and the tinsel for the Christmas tree which were in the bag she was carrying. "Come along," called Tony. "You can look at them properly when we get home."

"Do let's blow up one of the balloons now," begged Carol.

"Oh, all right," agreed Tony. He pulled out a big yellow one and began to puff hard into it. Then he found a piece of string in his pocket to tie round it.

"Isn't it a super one?" cried Carol.

"Oh, my," said a voice above them. "That's a lovely big moon you've got!" They looked up, and there was an elf sitting on a branch of a tree.

"It's not a moon, it's a balloon," explained Tony, and he threw the balloon up in the air so that the elf could look at it.

"Well, it looks like a moon," replied the elf. "I'll swap you a wish for it."

"Shall we?" Tony asked Carol.

"Yes," Carol replied. "It would be exciting to wish for something very special."

"Done!" said the elf. "Now what would you like to wish for?"

"I know what I'd like," said Carol. "Could you make it snow for Christmas?"

"Yes," the elf told her. "But we shall have to go up to Cloudland and see the snow fairies. Close your eyes and wish."

So Tony and Carol closed their eyes tightly and wished hard. Then they could feel the wind lifting them up and up.

"Very easily," replied the snow fairies. So they opened the gates of Cloudland and pushed the snowclouds across the sky.

"Come along," said the elf. "We'll go back to the wood now." Tony and Carol closed their eyes tightly and the wind took them down and down until they were back in Holly Lane.

"The snowflakes are beginning to fall already," cried the elf. "I'm going to show my friends my special moon. Goodbye!" And off he ran with the yellow balloon bobbing behind him.

Tony and Carol waved goodbye and then hurried all the way back home through the snow, to put up their decorations ready for Christmas.